Mrs. Noodlekugel

Mrs. Noodlekugel

Daniel Pinkwater

illustrated by
Adam Stower

CANDLEWICK PRESS

Text copyright © 2012 by Daniel Pinkwater
Illustrations copyright © 2012 by Adam Stower

First edition 2012

Library of Congress Cataloging-in-Publication Data

Pinkwater, Daniel Manus, date.
Mrs. Noodlekugel / Daniel Pinkwater ; illustrations by Adam Stower. — 1st ed.
p. cm.
Summary: Nick and Maxine have a new babysitter — the eccentric Mrs. Noodlekugel who lives in the funny little house behind their drab high-rise apartment building along with her feline butler, Mr. Fuzzface, and four farsighted mice.
ISBN 978-0-7636-5053-7
[1. Babysitters — Fiction. 2. Humorous stories.] I. Stower, Adam, ill. II. Title.
PZ7.P6335Mr 2012
[Fic] — dc22   2010048212

12 13 14 15 16 17 BVG 10 9 8 7 6 5 4 3 2 1

Printed in Berryville, VA, U.S.A.

This book was typeset in Esprit.
The illustrations were done in ink.

Candlewick Press
99 Dover Street
Somerville, Massachusetts 02144

visit us at www.candlewick.com

For Jill, who knew Mrs. Noodlekugel well
D. P.

For Norah, Florence, and Grace
A. S.

Nick

Maxine

Their Parents

A tall building, with one apartment stacked on top of another — that is where Nick and Maxine came to live with their parents. They had not lived there very long when Maxine said to Nick, "Come to my room. I have discovered something."

"What?" Nick asked. "What have you discovered?"

"You can see it out the window," Maxine said. "But you have to stand with your head in that corner."

"But there is a chest of drawers in that corner," Nick said.

"I know there is," Maxine said. "You have to stand on top of the chest of drawers and lean your head into the corner and look out the window and down. Then you will see it."

"Is that how *you* saw it? What were you doing standing on top of the chest of drawers?"

"Just do it. Tell me what you see."

Nick climbed onto the chest of drawers. He leaned his head into the corner.

He looked out the window and down.

"I see grass. I see trees and flowers. There is a little old-fashioned house."

"It is nice," Maxine said. "The house is cute. Did you know there was a backyard to this building with a cute little house in it?"

"I did not," Nick said. "We should go down there."

"Yes," Maxine said. "How do we get there?"

"I don't know," Nick said. "The whole street is tall apartment buildings, one after another, side by side. I don't know how to get to the back."

"I suppose it would not be a good idea to lower a rope out the window and climb down," Maxine said.

"There might be an easier way," Nick said. "We should ask someone."

"Could we ask Mike the janitor?"

"Yes. That is a good idea. Let's ask Mike the janitor."

Chapter 2

Mike the janitor mopped the floors and carried out the garbage and fixed things around the apartment building. Nick and Maxine knew him. He had a blue chin and a mustache like a brush, and he talked to himself. He was friendly to children. When he was not working around the building,

Mike the janitor sat in a little room in the basement, eating stewed tomatoes out of a can, talking to himself, and listening to the radio.

"Mike the janitor, how do we get to the backyard, and why is there a little house in it, and who lives there?" Nick and Maxine asked.

"The little house was built long before the apartment buildings," Mike said. "The buildings went up all around, and the house is where it always was. Mrs. Noodlekugel lives in the house. She is a nice old lady. You can get to the backyard by going through the boiler room, but do not tell your parents I told you."

Nick and Maxine did not tell their parents what Mike the janitor had told them. Just the same, later that same day, their father said, "Do not bother the old lady who lives in the back."

"Is she a witch?"

"No, she is not a witch. She is an old lady who lives in the little house, and you should not bother her."

"Do not go into the garden or onto the porch of the old lady who lives in the back," their mother said.

"Does she hate all children?"

"No, she does not hate all children. She is an old lady who lives in the little house, and you are not to go into her garden or onto her porch."

Chapter 3

The next day, Nick asked Maxine, "Do you think we should visit her?"

"Yes. Let's. Maybe she is lonely and would like a visit."

"I wouldn't be surprised."

Nick and Maxine went to the boiler room in the basement. There were

lots of big pipes and tubes, and the
boiler that was big and hot and made
gurgling and hissing noises.

There was a door that opened into the backyard. It was grassy and green, with trees and flowers, and there was the little house with a garden in front, and a yellow fence.

"It is pretty here," Nick said.

"The house looks friendly," Maxine said.

"It does not look like a house a witch lives in," Nick said.

"It does not look like the house of someone who hates all children," Maxine said.

They pushed open the gate. The
garden had sunflowers—also tomatoes,
squash, and pumpkins. There was
a birdbath made of concrete, a little
statue of an elf, and a round mirrored
ball on a concrete stand. There were

also three birdhouses on tall sticks. On the porch, there were three chairs, a thermometer, an American flag, and a statue of a tall, skinny cat with one black ear and one white ear.

"Do you see a button to push for the doorbell?" Nick asked.

"I don't see one," Maxine said. "Maybe we should just knock."

"I will see if the mistress is at home," a voice said. It was the cat statue. The statue stretched, pushed a little cat flap in the door, and disappeared into the house.

"It was a real cat!" Maxine said.

"And it talked!" Nick said.

"I don't think so," Maxine said. "Cats can't talk."

"But we heard it," Nick said.

"Maybe the lady is a ventriloquist," Maxine said. "Maybe it was a recording. We couldn't have heard the cat talk, because cats don't."

The door opened. There was a little old lady with bright dark eyes, a pointy little nose, and rosy cheeks. "Of course cats can talk," she said. And if someone is patient and takes the time to teach them, they can speak perfectly."

Chapter 4

Nick and Maxine could smell something delicious baking.

"Have you children come to visit me?" the old lady asked. "My name is Mrs. Noodlekugel, and what are your names?"

Nick and Maxine told Mrs. Noodle-kugel their names.

"Now that we have introduced ourselves, please come in and have some apple cookies," Mrs. Noodlekugel said. "Mr. Fuzzface — that is the name of my cat — baked them."

"Your cat can bake cookies?"

"Mr. Fuzzface is a very good baker. All Danish blues are."

"Danish blues?" Maxine asked.

"That is the type of cat he is," Mrs. Noodlekugel said. "The Danish blue, a very rare breed. And quite intelligent. Mr. Fuzzface is also an expert dancer, and he is teaching himself to play the piano."

"Do the children want milk with their apple cookies, or tea?" Mr. Fuzzface called from the kitchen. "Because I don't think we have enough milk."

"Tea will be fine," Maxine and Nick said.

"With lemon?" Mr. Fuzzface called.

"That will be fine, too," the children said.

Almost as surprising as a cat that talked was Mr. Fuzzface carrying a tray of cookies, then the teapot and cups, and arranging them on the table.

"Mr. Fuzzface is a very capable cat," Mrs. Noodlekugel said.

"We see that," Nick and Maxine said.

"Shall I call the mice?" Mr. Fuzz-face asked.

"Yes," Mrs. Noodlekugel said. "The children will enjoy seeing the mice, and the mice will enjoy some crumbs."

"Mice are going to eat with us?" Nick and Maxine asked.

"Oh, it would not be a tea party without the mice," Mrs. Noodlekugel said.

Chapter

5

Four fat mice appeared and stood shyly in the doorway.

"Come in, come in!" Mrs. Noodle-kugel said. "We have visitors! And cookies!" To Nick and Maxine she said, "All these mice have won prizes. They are prize-winning mice."

"I didn't know they gave prizes to mice," Nick said.

"Oh, they do! They do!" Mrs. Noodlekugel said.

The mice scampered up the tablecloth and sat in a row at the edge of the table. Mrs. Noodlekugel tore a paper napkin into four squares and handed them to the mice, who tucked them under their chins.

"Mr. Fuzzface came to me when I was working on the railroad," Mrs. Noodlekugel said. "He was a railroad cat. In those days, he could not speak a word of English, could you, Mr. Fuzzface?"

"Not a word," Mr. Fuzzface said.

"And you taught him to speak?" Nick asked.

"She did," Mr. Fuzzface said. "She was very patient. Cats have trouble with consonants, you see."

"I gave him exercises," Mrs. Noodlekugel said.

"Exercises?" Maxine asked.

"I had to say 'jingle jungle jangle joker' one hundred times," Mr. Fuzzface said. "And 'monkeys make Monopoly monotonous.'"

"And now he speaks perfectly!"
Mrs. Noodlekugel said.

"You are too kind," Mr. Fuzzface said.

While she was talking, Mrs. Noodlekugel poured out cups of tea for Nick and Maxine and tiny cups the size of thimbles for the mice. Mr. Fuzzface handed cookies round and broke off small pieces for the mice.

The children noticed that the mice appeared to have trouble finding the pieces of cookie — they had to sniff with their noses and feel around with their tiny fingers. And when they broke off crumbs to eat, they went to put them in their noses and eyes as often as into their mouths.

"The mice are farsighted," Mrs. Noodlekugel said. "But they enjoy tea parties."

Chapter 6

After a while, Maxine said, "We had a nice time."

"Thank you for the tea and cookies," Nick said.

"We should be going now," Maxine said.

"It was a pleasure to have you," Mrs. Noodlekugel said. "Please come back tomorrow and help us make gingerbread mice."

"We would love to come back tomorrow and make gingerbread mice," Nick and Maxine said. "Only . . ."

"Only . . . ?"

"Only our parents specifically told us not to bother you," Maxine said.

"Well, you have not bothered me, not in the least. I am happy to have you visit me."

"Still . . ." Maxine said.

"Still . . ." Nick said.

"You just tell them we had a nice visit, and you are invited to come tomorrow and make gingerbread mice," Mrs. Noodlekugel said.

Chapter 7

Nick and Maxine told their parents, "You know the old lady who lives in the little house in the back?"

"Yes," their parents said.

"Her name is Mrs. Noodlekugel, and she is not a witch," Nick said.

"We never thought she was a witch," their parents said.

"She does not hate all children," Maxine said.

"We never thought she hated all children," their parents said.

"Although you told us not to bother her, Maxine and I visited her anyway," Nick said.

"We thought you would," their parents said.

"She is nice," Maxine said.

"We know she is nice."

"She said we did not bother her in the least."

"Good. We are glad."

"Mrs. Noodlekugel says we can come tomorrow. We are going to make gingerbread mice."

"That will be fine," Nick and Maxine's parents said. "You may go."

"It will? We may?"

"Mrs. Noodlekugel is your new babysitter," Nick and Maxine's parents said. "When we have to be away, you are to go to the little house in the back, and Mrs. Noodlekugel will look after you."

"You knew that when you told us not to bother her," Nick said.

"Yes, we did."

"Did Mike the janitor tell you we were asking about the little house in the back?"

"Maybe."

"So, you are sneaky parents," Maxine said.

"You are tricky," Nick said.

"Yes, we are. Do you mind?"

"Well . . ." Nick said.

"Well . . ." Maxine said.

"Since we like Mrs. Noodlekugel, and Mr. Fuzzface and the four farsighted mice, and since we are going to learn to make gingerbread mice tomorrow, we don't mind at all."

Chapter 8

Mr. Fuzzface had on a white apron, and a white chef's hat. Mrs. Noodlekugel had a flowered apron.

"Here are aprons for you, children," Mrs. Noodlekugel said. "You may help me mix the gingerbread dough."

Nick and Maxine helped Mrs. Noodlekugel measure flour, molasses, butter, and ground ginger into a big bowl, also brown sugar and cinnamon. Then they took turns mixing with a big wooden spoon.

"I will add salt, an egg, and baking powder," Mr. Fuzzface said.

"Mix it well! Mix it well!" Mrs. Noodlekugel said.

"Now it is time to roll out the dough," Mr. Fuzzface said. "Then I will call the mice."

"What will the mice do?" Maxine asked.

"We will show you," Mrs. Noodlekugel said. "Mr. Fuzzface, please call the mice."

The four mice scrambled up onto the kitchen table.

"Now the mice will lie down on the cookie dough," Mrs. Noodlekugel said. "And we will trace around the mice with toothpicks. This way we will have mouse-shaped cookies. Be careful not to tickle the mice, children. They are quite ticklish."

Maxine and Nick traced around the mice with toothpicks. The mice giggled. Mrs. Noodlekugel took the mouse-shaped pieces of dough and put them on a big metal cookie sheet.

The mice themselves made cookie shapes, but they were so farsighted that the shapes did not look like mice. They looked like blobs.

"The outlines of mice the children made with toothpicks will be gingermice," Mrs. Noodlekugel said. "And the cookies the mice have made will be gingerblobs."

"Is this sanitary?" Nick asked.

"What do you mean?" Mrs. Noodlekugel asked.

"I mean, we are going to eat cookies made from dough that had mice lying on it," Nick said.

"Oh, we will not eat the gingermice, only the gingerblobs," Mrs. Noodlekugel said. "The gingermice are just for fun."

"So, we will not eat cookies made from dough that had mice lying on it, but it is OK to eat cookies mice made with their paws?" Nick asked.

"Mr. Fuzzface, did the mice wash their paws before making cookies?" Mrs. Noodlekugel asked.

"What?" Mr. Fuzzface said.

Chapter 9

Now we will put the cookies in the oven," Mrs. Noodlekugel said. "Before we light the oven, we will count the mice to make sure no mouse has fallen asleep on the cookie sheet."

"Has that ever happened?" Maxine asked.

"No, because we count," Mrs. Noodlekugel said.

"The mice are all present and correct," Mr. Fuzzface said.

"While the cookies are baking, perhaps Mr. Fuzzface would care to entertain us at the piano," Mrs. Noodlekugel said.

Mr. Fuzzface sat at the piano. "I am self-taught," he said.

Mr. Fuzzface played the piano fairly well, for a cat. He only knew one tune, "Three Blind Mice." He also sang, but he sang the words "four blind mice." He played and sang it over and over.

The mice applauded continually and jumped up and down.

Mrs. Noodlekugel tapped her foot and rocked in a rocking chair. Nick and Maxine tried to look pleased.

The little house began to smell wonderfully of baking gingerbread.

The cookies are done!" Mrs. Noodle-kugel said after a while. "Now they have to cool. We will decorate them with sugar frosting and raisins, and then we can eat the blobs and enjoy the scampering."

"Scampering?"

"You will see."

Decorating the gingermice and gingerblobs was fun. Nick and Maxine did some excellent decorations, as did Mr. Fuzzface and Mrs. Noodle-kugel. The cookies and blobs decorated by the mice made no sense at all because they were so farsighted.

"They are finished!" Nick and Maxine said.

"Not quite," Mrs. Noodlekugel said. "Just watch for a bit."

Nick and Maxine watched.

"Is that gingermouse moving?" Nick asked.

"And that one! I am sure I saw it move!" Maxine said.

In another moment, all the ginger-mice were moving. They scampered all over the kitchen table. They spun like tops. They jumped up and down. Mr. Fuzzface, Mrs. Noodlekugel, and the four mice clapped their hands and paws and were delighted.

Nick and Maxine were amazed.

"How is this possible?" Nick asked.

"Why is it happening?" Maxine asked.

"Mr. Fuzzface, do we know why the gingermice scamper?" Mrs. Noodlekugel asked.

"No, we do not," Mr. Fuzzface said. "I don't think we ever knew."

"It is just something that happens," Mrs. Noodlekugel said.

The gingermice scurried down the legs of the kitchen table and scurried out into the garden.

"Where are they going? What will happen to them?" Nick and Maxine asked.

"I do not know," Mrs. Noodlekugel said. "I suppose the crows will eat them."

"Eat them!"

"They are cookies," Mrs. Noodlekugel said.

"But they can move!"

"Yes! Isn't it entertaining?"

"Well, yes. It is extremely entertaining — and weird."

"We think so, too. Now, would you like tea with your gingerblobs?"

Mrs. Noodlekugel's
entertaining adventures
continue in

Mrs. Noodlekugel
and Four Blind Mice

Coming in 2013!